# It Came From The Cafeteria

Other books by Peter Lerangis

*Spring Fever!*

# IT CAME FROM THE CAFETERIA

## PETER LERANGIS

AN
**APPLE**
PAPERBACK

SCHOLASTIC INC.
New York Toronto London Auckland Sydney

ISBN 0-590-93970-X

12 11 10 9 8 7 6 5 4 3 2 1          6 7 8 9/9 0 1/0

Printed in the U.S.A.                                    40

First Scholastic printing, September 1996

*For the Jolly Authors' Group:*
*Barbara, Bonnie, Ellen, Fran,*
*Marvin, Miriam, and Sandra*
*— and, of course, the Empire Szechuan*

# It Came From The Cafeteria

# 1

*Mom . . . Dad?*

*Ethan Krantz tried to shout the words, but nothing came out of his mouth.*

*His lungs were screaming at him. Aching for air. Ready to burst.*

*He was tumbling, head over heels. On one side of him was a flaming, glowing mass. On the other, blackness.*

*Then the rumble started. And he heard a muffled, distant voice:*

*"Biiiiig baaanng . . ."*

*Oh, great.*

*That's where he was. At the big bang. At the beginning of the universe.*

*Just what he needed. One more thing to worry about.*

*"BIIIIG BAAAAANNNNNG!"*

*He felt himself tilting toward the hot, pulsating core. Grasping wildly at nothing . . .*

Good-bye Mom and Dad, *he thought.* Who knows? Maybe we'll meet again in a few hundred billion years or so . . .

*And then, a sharp thunder crack. Ethan's body gave a sudden jolt. And he felt himself falling. Falling fast . . .*

# 2

*W*HACK!
   "Yeeeeeow!" Ethan cried out.

He was sitting on the floor. Mr. Mosswort loomed overhead. Through his thick glasses, his eyes looked like trapped fish.

Mr. Mosswort lifted his yardstick off the long, black lab table. "Ahem. Welcome to the universe, Mr. Krantz. Do you have any idea what we've been talking about?"

"Uh . . . the big bang theory?" Ethan said, scrambling back onto his seat.

"Which is . . . ?" Mr. Mosswort replied.

Ethan swallowed deeply. What a way to begin the year. Falling asleep during bio lab, and it was only September fifth, the third day of school.

The entire class was staring at him. Twenty-five geniuses. The cream of the seventh grade at Eulenspiegel Middle School for Math and Science.

A fool. A total nincompoop. That's what Ethan felt like.

3

"Uh . . ." Ethan said. "Like, a big explosion in outer space? With atoms and stuff?"

"*Atoms and stuff?*" To Ethan's right, Hardy Fledermaus was roaring with laughter.

Mr. Mosswort scowled at him. "All right, Hardy, perhaps you can summarize for Sleeping Beauty what we've discussed?"

Hardy stood. His deep brown eyes scanned the room. He ran his fingers through his long, shoulder-length hair. Girls and guys both looked at him with quiet respect.

Ethan felt his stomach turn. Hardy was the Egomaniac of Eulenspiegel. The lead singer and songwriter of a heavy-metal band called Smashed Brains. Of which Hardy was the only member, so far.

"Actually, I've been working on some slam poetry about this very thing." Hardy began tapping his desk in rhythm. "The big bang. Cosmic clang. Hole of black, take it back. Back into time, gas and slime . . ."

*Make me puke*, Ethan thought.

"Very . . . creative," Mr. Mosswort said. "Who can put it into sentences?"

"Oooh! Oooh!" Hands shot up all over the room.

"Cecelia?" Mr. Mosswort asked.

To Ethan's left across the lab bench, Cecelia Myosis stood up. For a nanosecond, her soft blue eyes looked over toward him. He could feel the

4

glance on the side of his neck, like the brush of an eyelash.

For a nanosecond, Ethan forgot about his horrible daydream. He forgot about Hardy. He felt tingly right down to his toenails.

*Stop it*, Ethan said to himself. *She's a mutant egghead, like the rest of them.*

"The universe," Cecelia announced to the class, "can be explained as a point origin of mass and energy, collapsed inwardly to infinite density, which, having reached a critical point, then exploded, releasing the mass in an ever-expanding spray."

Ethan dropped his pencil.

"Did you understand any of that, Ethan?" Mr. Mosswort asked.

"Some of it," Ethan replied. "Like 'a' . . . 'then' . . . 'to' . . . 'in' . . ."

Mr. Mosswort slammed his ruler on his desk. "You can start by taking notes!"

Ethan quickly picked up his pencil and began scribbling the name CECELIA on a sheet of paper.

"So," Mr. Mosswort said, "what happened after the big bang — Benito?"

"First, balls of gas went flying through the cosmos," Benito Putterman said.

"Sounds like the cafeteria after lunch," Hardy muttered.

Ethan burst out laughing.

"Ethan!" Mr. Mosswort shouted. "What happened after these balls of gas formed stars and planets? How did life come about?"

"Life?" Gulp. What a question. "You mean, like, humans? Well, I guess, you know, these monkeyish creatures were hanging out, and —"

"Furry rodentlike mammalian precursors whose evolution was suppressed during the Mesozoic Era!" shouted Benito.

"They evolved from water-breathing invertebrates," Hardy said.

"And before that, unicellular cytoplasmic organisms!" Cecelia volunteered.

"Uh, yeah," Ethan said, "all that, too."

Mr. Mosswort exhaled with frustration. Grabbing a piece of chalk, he scribbled on the blackboard. "Boys and girls, each and every one of us comes from this."

Ethan tried to read the word:

*soup*

"We're descended from soap?" Ethan asked.

"*Soup*, Ethan!" Mr. Mosswort bellowed. "Not *soap*. We all come from a vast sea of primordial soup."

PRIME ORDEAL SOUP, Ethan wrote in his notebook.

"Does anyone know what that means?" Mr. Mosswort asked.

6

"Like, soup left over from a big ordeal?" Ethan said.

"EHHHHH!" Hardy made a noise like a game show buzzer. Around Ethan, the whole class was giggling.

Mr. Mosswort glared at him. *"Primordial.* It means 'the very first.' Before life as we know it. A sea of elements — oxygen, hydrogen, carbon, nitrogen — all boiling together in a wild, tumultuous soup."

Ethan felt his eyelids growing heavy again.

Mr. Mosswort pointed to a few bottles on his desk. "Ammonia, charcoal, water, soil. These were our ancestors. First came the simple, single-cell life forms. Then, over billions of years, a chain of evolution that led to humans!"

PEOPLE COME FROM SOUP, Ethan wrote in his notebook. Then he added, THIS IS RIDICULOUS.

"At the start of tomorrow's class, we will visit Eulenspiegel's enclosed environment, the famous Ecobubble," Mr. Mosswort said. "There, the eighth grade has been trying to duplicate the atmosphere that existed at the dawn of life . . ."

As Mr. Mosswort droned on, Hardy was scribbling furiously. His face was growing red, his features all scrunched up in a super-serious expression. Every few seconds he'd glance at Cecelia across the lab table.

Finally he folded his paper into a triangular

shape and gave it to Ethan. "Pass this to Cecelia," he whispered.

"I'm not your messenger!" Ethan hissed.

"Just do it!" Hardy insisted.

"AHEM!" Mr. Mosswort was now charging down the aisle. "Give me that!"

"But it's not —" Ethan began.

"Your notes, I presume, Ethan?" Mr. Mosswort grabbed the note, opened it, and read aloud:

" 'To Cecelia, the best girl in Eulenspiegel,
Your hair smells nice, not at all like a beagle.
When I'm not with you, my spirits droop;
My brain turns into primordial soup.
Yo, you are all right, Cecelia.
If you were a pear, I'd wanna peel ya.' "

"But — but I didn't —" Ethan sputtered.

He couldn't even hear himself. The class was howling with laughter.

Cecelia slumped into her chair, her face beet red.

Ethan looked at Hardy. But he was already heading for the door.

*RRRRRRINNNNG!* went the bell for the end of class.

Ethan slunk away. He felt about two inches tall.

8

# 3

"That was a nice poem."

At the sound of the familiar voice, Ethan spun around.

Cecelia Myosis was approaching, practically floating down the sidewalk.

Ethan's knees buckled. He nearly fell over. "Hi," he squeaked.

"Walking home?"

"Uh-huh."

"I'll walk with you."

Ethan felt as if his legs were made of whipped cream. But he managed to stay up as they fell in step together.

"Do I really make you feel like primordial soup?" Cecelia asked.

"Well, actually," Ethan said, "I didn't —"

"Kids here don't usually write poetry."

Ethan laughed. "I figured that out. But really, it wasn't —"

"You're not one of the test kids, are you? You know, the ones who passed the admissions test to get into Eulenspiegel, like me?"

"No," Ethan said with a sigh. "I'm here because my mom and dad were moved here by the government. They're geologists, working on some secret project."

Cecelia nodded knowingly. "The nuclear waste?"

"Huh?"

"In the ground. Didn't you know? Eulenspiegel used to be a nuclear dump."

"No way. My parents wouldn't have moved here if that were true!"

"Look at an old map. You don't see the name Eulenspiegel. Just 'Classified Government Compound.' No one came near here for thirty years, until some real estate people financed this big cleanup."

"But everything's okay now?" Ethan asked.

Cecelia smiled. "Ask your parents."

"Well, I don't see any radioactive mutants walking around."

"Take a look at the plants and grass around your house when you go home," Cecelia said. "Not to mention the insects."

"Why should I — ?"

"I love pears," Cecelia suddenly said.

"Uh . . . pears?"

"Mmmm. What did you mean when you wrote, 'If you were a pear, I'd wanna peel ya'?"

"Well, that's what I wanted to tell you. You see, I didn't really —"

"Ethan! Ethan, look!" a distant voice called.

A half-block ahead, Ethan's six-year-old brother was running across the Krantz front yard. He was holding something in his palm.

"What is it, Frodo?" Ethan asked.

"Check this out. It is sooooo cool!"

Frodo ran up to Ethan and Cecelia and opened his palm. On it was a grasshopper with a head on each end and two pairs of opposite-facing hind legs.

Frodo touched it gently. It hopped straight up. "You see?" Frodo said. "Both legs hop at the same time, so it can't move forward or back!"

Ethan felt a shiver. He looked over Frodo's shoulder at the house.

The grass that he had cut the day before was now ankle-high.

"So long," Cecelia said with a chuckle as she walked away. "And welcome to Eulenspiegel!"

# 4

The next day, Hardy was waiting for Ethan at the front door. "So, you think my poem needs work?"

"She thinks I wrote it," Ethan said, walking past him, toward the football field.

"Hey, where are you going?"

"To the Ecobubble. Remember? We're going to see what the eighth-grade geniuses are doing today."

Hardy followed close behind him like a stray dog. "So, did you tell her who really wrote it? Huh? Huh?"

"Why should I?" Ethan snapped. "After the way you treated me in class yesterday?"

"Look, I put my heart and soul into that poem! Did you take all the credit?"

"She didn't let me get a word in edgewise! Besides, why would I take credit for that garbage?"

"Don't be cruel, Ethan. You and I have to stick

together. We're the only normal kids in this weird place."

"*We?*"

"Well, you're normal. I'm close, because even though I'm a math genius, I have superior skills in the creative arts and rugged good looks."

Ethan laughed. "Modest, too."

"Hey, you think it's easy trying to be a rock star in this den of nerds? Okay, look, I have to let you in on a secret, Ethan. I've thought about this long and hard, and I have come to the conclusion that I need a muse. Someone to give me ideas. And you are it."

"What are you talking about?"

"Don't thank me. It's necessary. Here in Eulenspiegel, you're my only key to the real world. Okay, I'm sorry I kidded you a little. I take it back. But you, Ethan — you have what I need. You talk like a dumb, average kid. As a rock balladeer, I have to know what normal kids feel."

Ethan stopped. To his right, a giant black disk slowly rotated, with a small graph next to it that said E.T. INDICATOR: EULENSPIEGEL MIDDLE SCHOOL LOOKS FOR SIGNS OF INTELLIGENT LIFE.

"Hardy, you see that graph? Well, it dips every time I pass by. I feel like an idiot here. You want some advice from me? Fine. Then give me something in return. You be my tutor. You teach me what all the mumbo jumbo means in class. In return, I'll be as average as you want."

Hardy smiled. "Cold."

"Cool," Ethan advised him.

"See? I'm already learning."

Ethan headed toward the Ecobubble. It was just beyond an oval Astroturf track, where a football field would normally be.

Outside it, a red-haired girl was putting on what looked like a space suit.

"Okay, let's start," Ethan said. "Ecobubble. What and why? Fifty simple words or less. Go."

"Um . . . artificial indoor environment. You can change the temperature, humidity, whatever. Right now, they're trying to adjust the atmosphere to the way it was five hundred million years ago. Then maybe we can find out how the primordial soup became life." Hardy grinned. "That was forty words."

"That's ridiculous," Ethan said. "How can anyone know what the atmosphere was like back then?"

The girl in the space suit turned. "By visiting."

"Huh?" Ethan said. "Who are you?"

"Philomena Capstan," the girl replied, shaking Ethan's hand. "And your name is . . . Jefferson?"

"No, Krantz. Ethan Krantz."

"You remind me very much of the young Thomas Jefferson. Except his teeth were worse. Oh, well, grab a suit from the pile. We've adjusted

14

the atmospheric nitrogen content to match those samples I took." She pointed to a group of glass vials, rubber-banded together on the ground. "You wouldn't believe how this atmosphere has affected the plant growth. In combination with the unusual Eulenspiegel soil, they are thriving!"

Ethan gave Hardy a look. Hardy circled his finger around the side of his head, as if to say, *Cuckoo.*

"What if we go in there without the suits?" Ethan asked.

"Don't try it," Phil replied. "When I experienced the prehistoric atmosphere, I almost died. My lungs were bursting. Methane, nitrogen, and foul sulphuric gases almost blinded me —"

"Sounds like the boys' room," Hardy said with a grin.

Phil's eyes went wide. "How did you know?"

"Know what?" Hardy asked.

"The precise place where I found the rip in the space-time continuum," Phil replied.

"What are you talking about?" Ethan said.

"My water-pressure-activated intra-chronological navigator."

Ethan and Hardy just stared.

Phil rolled her eyes. "My time machine!"

"A time machine, in *the boys' room?*" Hardy asked.

Phil looked nervously over her shoulder. "You never heard me say that."

15

Donning a helmet, she stepped into the Eco-bubble.

"Insane," Ethan murmured.

Hardy held one of the vials up. He twisted off the top and took a whiff.

Instantly his face went pale. "Auughhh! She *was* in the boys' room!"

Ethan quickly put on a space suit and walked inside the Ecobubble.

He was swallowed up in a gray mist. All around him were huge, monstrous-looking plants with thick, rubbery leaves. One of them had round baubles that looked like eyes.

As Ethan walked deeper into the fog, the baubles seemed to follow him.

"Hardy?" Ethan called out. "Phil?"

The sound was muffled within his helmet. No one would be able to hear him. He stepped back toward the door.

The plant bent toward him.

Ethan stopped. The plant stopped.

Slowly, with a barely audible *creeeeak*, two enormous leaves opened up.

Inside them were rows of pointed talons, dripping with milky liquid that sizzled as it landed on the ground.

Ethan's jaw dropped open in shock.

The plant lunged for his face.

# 5

"**Y**EEEEEAAAAAAAA!"

Ethan bolted for the door.

He passed Hardy on the way. "Woohoogohee?" came the muffled sound from Hardy's helmet.

"Stay away!" Ethan yelled, gesturing to the plant.

Hardy stepped closer to it.

The plant had retracted. It hung harmlessly in its pot.

Ethan bolted outside. He spent the rest of the visit outside the Ecobubble.

Twenty minutes later, the class emerged. No one had seemed to notice he'd been gone.

Except Hardy. As they took off their space suits, Ethan patiently explained to him what had happened.

Big mistake. Hardy started whooping with hysterical laughter.

Ethan stormed back to the bio lab with the rest of the class.

"Yo, Ethan! Wait up!" shouted Hardy.

*I will beg Mom and Dad to leave,* Ethan said to himself. *If that doesn't work, I will threaten to jump into the mouth of that plant.*

Weird. The whole place was weird.

Philomena. Hardy. Mr. Mosswort. Two-headed grasshoppers. Speed-grow grass. Carnivorous plants.

*Why hadn't anyone else seen the plant?*

"Ethan of courage, Ethan of power," Hardy chanted, "chased away by a man-eating flower."

Ethan tried to run ahead, but Hardy followed right behind him.

"When the plant raised up its ugly head," Hardy called out, "little Ethan turned and fled . . ."

"Some friend you turned out to be, Fledermaus," Ethan muttered.

"Here lies good old Ethan Krantz . . . friend and neighbor, food for plants . . ."

Ethan stormed into the lab. "Hardy, I saw it! I can't believe you didn't."

"Well, it was kind of cloudy in there," Hardy replied.

"Didn't you think the place was strange? Everything seemed alive! Like, *human* alive! It's the soil, I know it. Or the air. Or both."

"Hoo boy, Philomena must be rubbing off on you."

"Very funny!"

Ethan plopped down onto his stool at the lab table. As the rest of the class straggled in, he fiddled nervously with a bottle of ammonium sulfate. He picked fronds off an asparagus plant growing in a small pot. He tapped out a rhythm on a beaker of distilled water.

Cecelia sat on her stool across from him. "Hi, Ethan."

"Guess what?" Hardy said, leaning across the table with a slimy grin. "I was the one who wrote that poem."

Cecelia's face fell. "You did not. Ethan —"

"I passed it to him," Hardy explained. "You didn't think he had the talent to write something so polished?"

Cecelia gave Ethan a sharp look.

Ethan nodded sadly. "I tried to tell you on the way home from school."

"I worked all night at it," Hardy continued. "I was obsessed. See, I believe that writing is the window to a person's soul . . ."

Ethan was starting to feel nauseated again.

"I started with the image of primordial soup," Hardy went on. "I mean, it's just like real-life feelings. All those basic ingredients — hydrogen, nitrogen . . ." Hardy gathered a bunch of bottles together on the lab table. "They're just like the ingredients of people — looks, thoughts, lifestyle choices. You don't really notice them, until they

19

join together. Then they become something greater. Something beautiful."

"Beautiful..." Cecelia was looking at Hardy with rapt attention.

What a dork.

What a conceited, two-faced jerk.

Ethan was seeing red. "Basic ingredients, huh?" he blurted out. "Wow, how deep. Let's see how it works, Hardy. Let's see how you make your beautiful poetry."

One by one, Ethan uncapped the bottles. They were all full of chemicals.

"First... *looks*..." He poured some ammonia into an empty test tube.

"*Thoughts*..." Another bottle into the same tube.

"*Lifestyle choices*... lots of those..." Three more bottles.

"And for good measure, some nice, fast-growing Eulenspiegel soil." Ethan dug a spoon into the dirt of the asparagus plant and dumped some of that in, too.

Cecelia and Hardy were staring at him, astonished.

Ethan picked up the test tube. He put a cork stopper over the top and shook. "Now, let's see what we get! Instant primordial soup! As beautiful as Hardy's poetry."

With a grin, he took the stopper off.

Cecelia and Hardy turned white. Benito, who had just sat down, began gagging.

"Eeeeeewww!" screamed Shira Shamsky.

All around the room, kids were coughing and running for the door.

Ethan's eyes stung. The stench was like a punch to the face. Like sticking your face into the sewer.

"KRAAAAANTZ!" Mr. Mosswort shouted. "You remove that smell from this room right away!"

Ethan grabbed the stopper and stuffed it into the top of the test tube. Around him, the class was racing to the windows and yanking them open.

Ethan jumped to his feet and ran out of the room.

The last thing he saw was a look of utter disgust on Cecelia's face.

# 6

*Q*UOOOOOOOOOOOOOSH!
The toilet must have been broken. Its never-ending flush was the only sound Ethan heard in the boys' room.

He held the stoppered test tube tightly. No smell was escaping. Good.

Quickly he peeked around. No one at the sinks or anywhere else. Also good.

The door to the broken toilet was closed, but the next one was open, so Ethan ducked in.

Dump it, flush, and run. In a minute he'd be rid of this vile stuff.

He held his breath and unstoppered the test tube.

As he lifted the seat, he noticed a large sign bolted to the wall:

WARNING!
THIS IS A SANITARY FACILITY!
NO DISPOSING OF PAPER TOWELS
OR LABORATORY CHEMICALS!

Ethan quickly popped the stopper back on.

He let out his breath. The leftover fumes nearly knocked him out.

This was stupid! How else was he supposed to get rid of this stuff? What was wrong with a few stinky chemicals in the sewer system?

Ethan put the test tube in his back pocket, left the stall, and headed for the hallway door.

*QUOOOOOOOOOOOOOOSH!*

Boy, was that noise obnoxious. And what a waste of water. A whole school of science geniuses, and no one could fix the john?

Well, Ethan could. He'd done it in his house. How hard could this one be?

He went to the stall and leaned against the door. It wouldn't budge.

He knocked. "Anyone in there?"

*QUOOOOOOOOOOOOOOSH!* was his answer.

He pushed again, with all his weight. No luck.

Ethan sighed. Some things just had to be done the hard way.

He walked to the other end of the bathroom and rolled up his sleeves. Then he sprinted toward the door, his shoulders down.

Just before he reached it, it flew open.

Ethan jammed on the brakes. He tried to dig his heels into the tile floor.

And a dark, bearded man jumped out at him!

# 7

"AAAAAAAAGGH!" Ethan sprang back. "AAAAAAAAAAGGH!" screamed the man.

Ethan pressed himself against the wall. The toilet had stopped flushing. In the sudden silence, he could hear his own panicked breathing.

The stranger was short and thin, and he wore a floppy hat that came down over his eyes. "Sorry!" he squeaked. Then he cleared his throat and deepened his voice: "I mean, sorry."

Ethan looked closely at the waxy black beard. "Who are you?"

"I'm, um, the father of one of the students. Well, got to go!"

As the man turned, Ethan caught a glimpse of the bright red hair under the hat. "Philomena?"

"Arrrrgh." Philomena ripped off her beard. "How did you know?"

"What's with the disguise? What are you doing here?"

Phil hung her head. "Camouflage. It's the only way I can get in here without drawing attention."

"Why don't you use the girls' room?"

"My experiment only works here."

Ethan remembered their conversation outside the Ecobubble. He pointed to the stall. "Don't tell me. Is that —?"

"My water-pressure-activated intra-chronological navigator?" Phil said. "Yes."

Ethan peered in. "Looks like a toilet to me." *Looney farm*, he thought. *Where's the sign-up sheet?*

"It's no ordinary toilet," Phil said. "It just happens to be located at the wormhole flux point —"

"There are *worms* in there?"

"A wormhole in time! Don't you know a thing about cosmology?"

"I'm a guy! I don't use makeup!"

"That's cosmetology." Phil rolled her eyes. "This, Ethan Krantz, is the precise area of a natural time-space confluence!"

Ethan nodded. "I get confluence all the time, especially when I eat dried fruits."

"Do you realize what a discovery this is?" Phil barreled on. "Here, the earth's magnetic and gravitational forces create a zone in which the stream of time and space are warped."

"So, you go in there, you flush, and *zoom*, back to the beginning of time?"

Phil burst out with sudden, hysterical cackling.

Ethan smiled. Okay, the joke was up. It was about time. Ethan was beginning to think Phil was seriously demented.

He joined in the laughter.

"You're like a quasar, Ethan," Phil said. "Interesting, but dense. How could I have gone back that far without an oxygen tank?"

"Right! Oxygen tank!" Ethan said, still laughing. "Good question!"

"No, just the Revolutionary War, I'm afraid." Phil reached into her pocket and took out a plastic bag full of leafy brown stuff. "They were throwing this tea off the dock. What a waste. I figured I'd sneak some back."

"Uh, Phil, the joke is kind of growing old, and I have to get back to —"

"I aimed for the landing on Plymouth Rock," Phil said with a sigh. "I'm still learning, I guess. The length of time travel seems to be affected by the length of the flush. The space-time rift is probably water-pressure sensitive, of course."

"Of course."

Phil giggled. "I guess you thought I was kind of wacko because of this disguise."

"Well, the disguise wasn't the main reason —"

*RRRRRING!*

Ethan groaned. "That's the bell! I was supposed to go back to bio!"

"Don't worry." Phil waved her hand dismissively. "I had Mosswort last year. He forgets you as soon as you leave the room. Come on, let's go to lunch."

"Okay."

As they walked toward the door, Phil asked, "What were you doing in here? I smelled something unbelievably foul as I was returning from Colonial New England."

"Will you stop with the time-travel stuff already?" Ethan said. "Anyway, this guy in bio named Hardy really gets on my nerves. So I got mad and started mixing these chemicals together — you know, just to make fun of something he was saying?"

"And you think *I'm* weird?"

"Well, you smelled how gross the stuff turned out. Mr. Mosswort told me to get rid of it."

Just as they reached the door, Hardy Fledermaus came barging in.

He stopped short when he saw Ethan and Phil. A smile crept across his face. "Who-o-o-o-oa, don't let me interrupt anything!"

"Clear, please," Phil said.

Hardy started beating a rhythm on the tile walls. "*Hel*lo, *E*than, *what's* going *on*? *Hi*din' with *Phi*-il *in* the *john* . . ."

"Knock it off, Fledermaus," Ethan said.

"*First* comes *love*, but *when's* the *mar*riage? . . . In the *eight*een *hun*dreds, with a *horse*-drawn *car*riage!"

Ethan and Phil stormed out of the bathroom.

27

The echo of Hardy's laughter followed them down the hallway.

"Creep," Ethan said.

"I'd rather walk upright, thank you," Phil replied.

"No. I mean, Hardy's a creep. I wish your time machine were real. Then he could flush it and become a lunch snack for a tyrannosaurus."

"Doubtful. For that you need the precise magnetic coordinates and flush-lever pressure. Not to mention the timing —"

"Yeah, right." Ethan took his test tube out of his back pocket. "I'll see you in the cafeteria. I have to put this outside in the Dumpster."

"Okay. 'Bye."

As Phil walked into the cafeteria, Ethan headed toward the school's side exit.

"Hooooo-ha-ha-ha-ha . . ." echoed Hardy's voice through the boys' room door.

Ethan stopped. To his right was a row of lockers. One of them was labeled H. FLEDERMAUS with a plastic strip of letters.

The vents on the locker were narrow. But they were plenty wide enough to pour liquid through.

Ethan grinned.

# 8

"**H**eyyy, Romeo! Where's your Juliet?" Hardy's voice thundered.

Yikes.

Ethan slipped the test tube back into his pocket. Lousy timing. He'd have to try again later.

He quickly headed into the cafeteria.

"Wait up!" Hardy said. "You're not mad at me, are you?"

"Cram it, Hardy," Ethan said.

Hardy pulled out a small notebook. " 'Cram it . . .' I like that expression. It has a good ring to it."

Ethan trudged toward the lunch line. *Just a split second later*, he thought. *A split second, and I could have made his life miserable.*

He grabbed a tray and slid it onto the metal ledge.

Just ahead of him, Benito Putterman had stopped in his tracks. "Ewwwww!" he screamed.

Ethan almost choked.

The stench around him was overpowering. He felt his test tube, thinking the stopper had popped off.

It hadn't.

"What *is* it?" asked Benito.

He was staring at the steam table. Mrs. Gastronome, the head of the lunch staff, was lowering a deep rectangular tray into its slot. In it was a stringy, boiling, dark-green substance. It was flecked with small brownish-white objects that bubbled to the surface and then submerged, like tiny, drowning insects.

"Spinach-garlic-garbanzo bean casserole," Mrs. Gastronome replied.

"We're supposed to eat that?" Benito said.

"I don't plan the menu, I just serve the food," Mrs. Gastronome snapped.

Ethan couldn't believe his nose. The stuff smelled almost as bad as his test-tube solution.

Benito grabbed a salad and bolted.

"Yo, Ethan!" Hardy was bouncing down the lunch line, sliding a tray. "Hey, I didn't mean to disk you."

"*Dis*," Ethan said, "as in *dis*respect."

"Right. It's just that, after you lied to Cecelia, I had a hard time —"

"I didn't lie!"

Hardy sniffed. "Is that spinach? Yum. I love spinach." Hardy held out his plate to Mrs. Gastronome. "I'll take some of that."

She looked up so fast, her glasses nearly fell off her face. "You *will?*"

"Hardy, you're sick," Ethan said.

Hardy shrugged. "My dad makes this all the time. What's the matter, not too many takers?"

"You're the first," Mrs. Gastronome said.

As she ladled a glob of the green stuff onto Hardy's plate, the other cafeteria workers gathered around to watch in awe.

Holding their noses, a group of kids stepped around Ethan and Hardy. They hightailed it to the cashier.

Ethan turned to follow but stopped. Out of the corner of his eye, he spotted Cecelia entering the lunch line.

Her face crinkled with disgust at the stink.

"Heyyyy!" Hardy called out. "It's cool Cecelia, Cecelia the Cool. Coolest girl in the whole wide school."

"Hi," Cecelia said with a warm smile. "That's so sweet."

"I taught him that word," Ethan blurted out. "*Cool*, I mean."

Cecelia looked at him blankly.

"Don't mind him," Hardy said. "He's a little depressed. His girlfriend just left to visit the Civil War."

"Cram it, Hardy," Ethan said.

Hardy winked at Cecelia. "He taught me that, too. Ethan is full of colorful expressions."

31

Cecelia laughed. "Hardy, you're weird."

"Ahh, that laugh . . . like the song of birds," Hardy recited. "Much more sweet than lying nerds." He glanced back at Ethan. "No offense."

Ethan was seeing red.

As Hardy blabbered more stupid rhymes to Cecelia, Ethan trained his eyes on Hardy's plate. On the greenish goop that was just sitting there. Sitting there and waiting.

Ethan reached into his pocket. His fingers closed around the test tube.

He popped off the top.

The familiar smell was there, but it was smothered by the cafeteria stench.

Hardy wouldn't notice a drop of solution in his food.

At least until he tasted it.

Heh-heh.

*Do it!* a voice screamed in Ethan's brain.

Nahhhhh. How could he? It was cruel. It was diabolical. It was inhuman.

Hardy was gesturing dramatically. "So come with me; let's sing and dance . . . forget your cares; say, 'Cram it, Krantz' . . ."

That did it.

With a flick of the wrist, Ethan dumped the entire contents of his test tube onto Hardy's plate.

"Ewwwwwww!" screamed another student, racing by.

"Uh, Hardy, what *is* that smell?" Cecelia asked.

Hardy turned around. "Lunch."

Cecelia took one look at the casserole in the steam table and blanched. "That is the most disgusting thing I have ever seen!"

Mrs. Gastronome pointed her thumb at Hardy. "His dad makes it all the time."

Hardy leaned forward, his body blocking his plate from Cecelia's view. "How dare you dish me?"

"Dis," Mrs. Gastronome reminded him.

"Mrs. Gastronome, you should be ashamed of yourself!"

With one hand, Hardy lifted his plate, still concealed from Cecelia behind his back.

As Ethan watched in horror, Hardy slid the spinach casserole back into the steam tray.

And the bio lab mixture with it.

# 9

"**N**o!" Ethan yelled.

Hardy, Cecelia, and Mrs. Gastronome all stared at him.

"You — you can't serve that stuff!" Ethan pleaded.

Mrs. Gastronome chuckled. "You're not the first one to tell me that."

"You don't understand," Ethan pleaded. "It's inedible. It contains a foul, smelly substance."

"Three of them," Mrs. Gastronome replied. "Spinach, garlic, garbanzo beans —"

"Not just them." Ethan took a deep breath. "I — I —"

The words caught in his throat. What could he say? *Uh, sorry, but I put some poisonous glop in the spinach?*

"I —"

But what if he didn't admit it? He could just picture the headlines: *TWELVE-YEAR-OLD BOY CONTAMINATES SCHOOL FOOD SUP-*

*PLY. GENIUSES RUSHED TO HOSPITAL IN CAFETERIA SABOTAGE.*

Another group of kids raced by, screaming, "EWWWWW!"

Cecelia was holding her nose. "Gaaaah, it smells worse by the minute!"

"Ethan, I don't think you need to worry," Mrs. Gastronome said drily. "No one will eat this."

"Come on, Ethan," Hardy said. "Stop slowing up the line."

Ethan gulped.

The casserole was starting to congeal. A grayish-brown film had formed on the top. Yellow crust rimmed the steel tray.

Mrs. Gastronome was right. No normal kid was going to touch the stuff. Especially with the added aroma.

But how many normal kids were in Eulenspiegel Middle School?

Ethan grabbed a tuna salad sandwich and a pudding and paid for his lunch.

"EWWWW!"

"Yeccch!"

"Gross!"

Behind him, the lunch line was ringing out with evaluations of the casserole.

Ethan eyed every plate in the cafeteria. Not one of them contained the dark-green glop.

Whew.

He headed for the far corner of the cafeteria.

Phil was sitting at a table there, hunched over a calculator. Her tray lay empty on the table beside her.

"Hi," Ethan said, sitting across from her. "Phil, what did you have for lunch?"

Phil glanced up. "A sandwich."

"None of the casserole?"

"Are you nuts?"

"Nope. Listen, Phil, can you keep a secret?"

"In the present, yes. But I reserve the right to tell anyone if I go into the past."

"Okay." Ethan lowered his voice to a whisper. "Remember that stuff in my test tube?"

"The primordial soup?"

"It's not primordial soup! It's just this mixture of chemicals from bio lab!"

Phil shrugged. "You never know."

"I'm serious, Phil!"

"Me, too."

"Well, it's in the spinach-garlic-garbanzo bean casserole now."

"*Whaaaaat?* Why did you do that?"

"I didn't! Hardy did!"

"Why'd he do it?"

"He didn't! I mean, he didn't know he was doing it. But it was in his portion, and he threw it back!"

Phil cocked her head curiously. "Ethan, are you feeling all right? You're not making any sense."

"Look, it doesn't matter how it happened. But I feel guilty about it, Phil. I don't want to tell the truth, because I'll get in trouble. But what if someone eats it?"

"EEEEEEEEEE!" came a scream from the lunch line.

Phil laughed. "You're worried?"

"That was an 'EEEE,' wasn't it? Not an 'EEEEEWW.'"

"So?"

"YEEEEEEEEEAAAAGGGGGHH!"

"Someone is screaming!" Ethan bolted to his feet and ran back toward the lunch line.

Three kids were running out, holding their noses. Behind them was Mrs. Gastronome. She backed into the doorway, holding a push broom. "Back! Back!" she yelled.

A blackish-green ooze crept toward her on the floor. Mrs. Gastronome tried desperately to sweep it away, but it lapped over the top of the broom.

Ethan froze.

Phil raced up behind him. "What happened?"

"It —" Ethan's throat was parched with fear. He could barely get the words out.

"It's . . . alive!"

# 10

*SCREEEEEE...*

Left and right, chairs scraped against the floor.

Kids gathered near Ethan and Phil, gawking. "Get it, Gastronome!" shouted Melvin Wattenmaker.

"I bet it slimes her!" Shira Shamsky replied.

"A pack of calculator batteries she wins!" cried Elmira Furd.

"Take *that*!" Mrs. Gastronome yelled. "And *that*!"

In the distance, Ethan heard a clomping noise like a charging elephant.

Mr. Sneed, the principal, came running in. His pot belly jiggled over his belt, and his bald pate was red from the effort. *"What is this commotion?"*

Mr. Schmutzkopf, the custodian, ran in behind him with a snow shovel. "Move, thunder drawers! Or go get me a pail!"

"Well — I never — who —" Mr. Sneed humphed.

Ethan sprang into action. He ran into the hallway and dragged in a big metal waste barrel.

Hardy and Cecelia rounded up two more.

They sped back into the kitchen.

What a mess.

The spinach-garlic-garbanzo bean casserole was bubbling over the steam table, spilling onto the floor.

"Out of the way!" Mr. Schmutzkopf yelled, brandishing his shovel. He elbowed aside the chef, who was pounding the casserole with a rolling pin.

"Mrs. Gastronome, I demand to know the meaning of this!" Mr. Sneed bellowed.

Mrs. Gastronome pushed against the oozing tide with all her strength. "We need..." she grunted, "to have a talk...about the menu!"

"Yeeeee-haaaaah!" screamed Hardy, dragging in a barrel. "Spinach, spinach, on the floor; clean it till your back is sore..."

"All Eulenspiegel students, back to your tables!" Mr. Sneed yelled.

A glob of slimy green pushed its way underneath him.

"Uh, Mr. Sneed...?" Benito said.

"Now!" Mr. Sneed thundered. He raised his foot and stamped it down.

*Plap!* The goo spat out from under his wing-tip shoe.

"Who-o-o-o-oa!"

Mr. Sneed went flying upward.

With a dull splat, his bottom landed square in the spinach-garlic-garbanzo bean casserole.

"HAAAAAAH!" Half the kids in the cafeteria fell to the floor in hysterics.

"Get more barrels!" Ethan cried out.

Cecelia and Philomena ran into the hallway, followed by a group of other kids.

Two assistant custodians were right behind, with more shovels.

*Splursh!*

*Glooop!*

*Flommmp!*

The custodians and kitchen workers dumped load after load of spinach-garlic-garbanzo bean casserole into the garbage barrels. Ethan, Cecelia, and Phil kept darting into the hallway, retrieving barrels from all over the school.

This was war.

A half hour later, Mr. Schmutzkopf scooped up the last remaining pile of glop. It quivered as it settled into the green mass in the garbage barrel.

With a loud *clomp*, Ethan brought the lid down.

By then, he, Phil, and Mr. Schmutzkopf were the only ones left in the cafeteria. Together they dragged the barrel into the school lobby.

There, in the middle of the entire student body and school administration, stood seven loaded garbage barrels. And Mr. Sneed, dressed in a dry, spare suit that was at least two sizes too small.

"Mr. Schmutzkopf!" he growled. "I demand you dispose of this now or I will have your job!"

*Rrrrrip!* His left pants leg split right up the seam.

"Uh, excuse me."

Mr. Sneed ran off, his pants leg flapping around his bare leg.

"To the incinerator!" Mr. Schmutzkopf yelled.

His work boots lifted high, Mr. Schmutzkopf stomped down the hallway toward the elevator.

Ethan and Phil followed, pulling a casserole-filled barrel. Cecelia and Hardy were behind them with another.

The hallways resounded with scraping noises all the way to the custodian's elevator.

Mr. Schmutzkopf rode down with the barrels. Everyone else took the stairs.

The incinerator furnace was at the end of a long corridor. Ethan helped take the barrels to Mr. Schmutzkopf and his assistants, who emptied them, one by one, into the roaring fire.

"Heave . . . ho!" shouted Mr. Schmutzkopf as he tossed in the last one.

A big cheer rang out.

The smell had disappeared. The crowd began heading back, everyone laughing and slapping high fives.

Ethan fell against a wall, exhausted.

"Are you okay?" Phil asked.

Ethan nodded. "I guess you were right, huh?"

"About what?"

"The primordial soup."

Phil laughed. "I was joking. You can't really make that stuff."

"Then what happened to the spinach-garlic-garbanzo bean casserole?"

"Who knows? Maybe an infusion of gas that gave the appearance of massive growth, or a liquefying agent that drew moisture and caused uncontrollable spillage . . . perhaps even some expansive reagent or —"

"We filled *seven barrels*, Phil — from one tray!"

*"Attention all Eulenspiegel Middle School students and administrative personnel!"* sounded Mr. Sneed's voice over the scratchy P.A. *"School is hereby dismissed until tomorrow!"*

Ethan could hear a dull roar of approval from the students upstairs.

*"And, uh, will anyone with a needle and thread please report to the principal's office immediately?"*

Phil put her arms around Ethan's shoulders. "Come. Let's go to the ice-cream shop for a cone and a nice chat about quantum physics."

"Maybe another day, Phil," Ethan said wearily. "But I'll walk home with you."

They trudged up the stairs and into the hallway.

Kids were racing around, grabbing coats and books out of lockers.

"Meet you in front of the school," Phil said, running off.

By the time Ethan reached his locker, the school had nearly emptied. He reached inside and took out his backpack.

Putting it on, he stretched and let out a yawn.

*Shhlooop.*

He snapped to attention. At the other end of the hallway, a sudden motion on the floor caught his eye.

Something was moving. It was about the size of a rat, but it had no legs. It slithered, like a snake.

And it seemed to leave a thin trail of slime.

As it disappeared around the corner, at the end of the hallway, Ethan caught a glimpse of its color.

Dark green.

# 11

**E**than blinked.

Could it have been a piece of the cafeteria glop? A small lump that got away?

Nahh, couldn't have been.

*Clank!*

His neck hairs pricked up.

The sound came from around the corner.

Probably someone closing a locker.

Ethan tiptoed down the hallway, staying near the wall. The only noise now was a faint buzzing from the overhead fluorescent light.

When he reached the corner, he slowly peered around.

The hallway stretched into the distance. Lockers lined both walls. A few sheets of paper and candy wrappers lay abandoned on the floor. A group of kids was heading away from Ethan, toward the EMS lobby.

To the left, a metal exit door stood ajar.

A thin, slimy trail led to it.

Ethan walked toward it, his eyes trained on the

floor. He pushed the door open. Just outside was a Dumpster, stuffed to the brim with garbage. Beyond that was the teachers' parking lot. In the distance to the right, the Ecobubble loomed over the school grounds.

Ethan scanned the area. He walked outside, circling slowly around the parking lot.

By the chain-link fence, he heard a sudden rustling sound.

He froze.

A small green tail shimmied briefly, then disappeared into the underbrush.

Ethan exhaled. It was a lizard. A harmless little lizard.

Of course. This was New Mexico. Reptile country. Reptiles slithered. Reptiles were green.

"Duh," Ethan said under his breath.

With a chuckle, he headed back to the school.

As he passed the Dumpster, he heard a muffled, thrashing noise. Like the rustling of papers and plastic.

He banged the side. "Having a nice lunch?"

The noise stopped.

Ethan giggled. He backed through the door, watching the Dumpster. Waiting to see a scared, scaly creature jump out.

The top of the Dumpster slowly started to lift. Ethan caught a glimpse of green.

Then, from behind him, a pair of hands clamped over his eyes.

# 12

"**Y**AAAAAGH!" Ethan shouted.

He spun around.

Philomena dropped her arms. "I was going to say, 'Guess who?'"

"*Why did you do that?*" Ethan yelled. "You nearly gave me a heart attack!"

"Well, *I* nearly died of boredom waiting for you in front of school. So we're even. What were you doing?"

"Looking for lizards," Ethan grumbled, walking toward the lobby.

Phil shook her head. "Ethan, you are strange."

"Look who's talking."

"No need to be nasty," Phil snapped. "You know, I don't *have* to walk home with you."

As they pushed their way through the front doors, Ethan sighed. "Sorry, Phil. I'm just upset."

"Love problems?" Phil asked.

"Love? *Me?*" Ethan chuckled. "What gave you that stupid idea?"

Phil shrugged. "I could see the way you were looking at Cecelia during lunch. And the way she wasn't looking at you."

"You really think you're smart, don't you? You think you have all the answers."

"Why don't you do something about it?"

"About what?"

"About Cecelia! Ask her out on a date."

Ethan glared at her. "I don't want to talk about this, Phil! I don't like girls!"

"Thanks a lot."

"I mean, like, I *like* them. Like I like you. But not, like, *like* like."

"I know exactly what you mean."

"You do?"

"Just call her," Phil said. "Look, I know her. She won't mind. Trust me on this one."

"No *way*!" Ethan stomped away in the direction of his house. "Never in a million billion years!"

*Five-five-five* . . .

Ethan double-checked the number in the phone book. Then he continued tapping it out.

*Eight-four-seven-nine.*

He cradled the receiver in his ear and sat back.

Outside the kitchen window, the house next door shone golden in the rays of the setting sun. The TV laugh track swelled and ebbed in the family room, like rolling ocean waves.

Mom, Dad, and Frodo were all in there, safely glued to sitcoms.

"Hello!" a deep voice boomed.

Ethan nearly jumped out of the seat.

"Hi thith is Etheilia is Cecelan home?" Ethan squeaked.

"Who?"

"*Cecelia!*" Ethan blurted out. "Is Ethan home?"

"Who's Ethan?"

"Me! May I seek to Specilia?"

"Ceceeeelia!" shouted the voice. "Some nutcase on the phone for you!"

*Hang up*, Ethan thought. *Hang up and forget the whole thing.*

"Hello?"

Too late.

Ethan's jaw felt like a jackhammer. "H — H — Hi, Cececececelia."

"Who is this?"

Ethan took a deep breath. It was now or never.

"Ethan Krantz. I was just calling — I wondered — Would you . . . ?" Ethan's throat dried up in mid-sentence.

"Would I what?"

"Help me with the math homework?"

*Ugh. Lame.* Ethan was cringing.

Cecelia laughed. "Uh, Ethan, there was no math, remember? We had a half-day."

"Oh. Okay. Well, then, I guess, 'bye."

" 'Bye."

48

"Oh, and I almost forgot," Ethan quickly added. "You don't want to go out, right? No? Well, that's okay —"

"Sure."

Ethan felt faint. "Sure?"

"Uh-huh. When? Now?"

"Uh . . ." Ethan looked at the kitchen clock. It read THURS SEP 6 7:08. The Thursday lineup of prime-time shows wouldn't be over until nine-thirty.

Until then, nobody would notice he was gone.

"Okay," Ethan said. "Great! See you!"

"Wait, Ethan! Where?"

"Oh! I don't know."

"Walk by my house. I'm at fifty-seven Roquefort Court."

"Okay, 'bye."

" 'Bye."

Ethan slammed the phone down. "Yyyyyyes!" He shouted toward the family room: "Mom? Dad? I'm going to stow away on a steamboat to the South Seas, jump ship, and live with dolphins!"

"Okay, son," his dad replied. "Have fun."

"Say hello from us," his mom added.

Just as he thought. Their minds were deep into prime time. He was free as a bird.

He raced outside and ran all the way to Roquefort.

Cecelia was waiting on her porch. "Hi!" she exclaimed.

"Hi," Ethan replied.

"It was really sweet of you to come and apologize," she said, walking toward the sidewalk.

"Apologize?"

"For lying about the poem, and for making all that smelly stuff. That is why you came over, right?"

"Uh, yeah! Exactly. Wow. I'm sorry."

"Phil said you were feeling so guilty, you were crying."

"I was?"

"She said you thought I'd never speak to you again, and that broke your heart."

"*Whaaaat?* I mean, *whaaaat* true words! Whew, was I sad!"

He made a mental note to thank Philomena and never again make fun of her dumb time-travel stories.

Cecelia took Ethan's arm. "Come on, let's go to the Double Helix for an ice cream."

Ethan was flying. He could not feel his feet touching the ground.

The Double Helix was in Eulenspiegel Center, just past the middle school. As Ethan and Cecelia turned off Roquefort and onto Edification Drive, the moon was rising over the school's roof, just ahead of them.

"Mmm, a waning gibbous," Cecelia said.

"Where?" Ethan looked around in a panic. "I hate monkeys."

50

"The *moon*, silly."

"There are monkeys on the moon?"

Cecelia giggled. "You know, you have a great sense of humor."

"Heh-heh," Ethan laughed cautiously.

They crossed the street and strolled past houses overgrown with grass and plants. Soon they were walking past EMS.

"What a strange day it was in school, huh?" Cecelia said.

Memories of the day flooded back into Ethan's head. The growing, bubbling casserole. The strange lizard.

"Cecelia," Ethan said, "have you ever seen a reptile about the size of a rat inside the school?"

"Nahhh. They stay outside."

*Clank!*

Ethan stopped.

"Did you hear that?"

"Yes." Cecelia was eyeing the parking lot. "I saw something move, too."

"Where?"

"Near the Dumpster. At the side of the school."

"I *knew* it!" Ethan exclaimed. "There *is* something in there! Come on!"

They both ran toward the parking lot.

Ethan slowed down just before the Dumpster. It was hidden in the shadow of an overhang, far from the only distant light that shone on the parking lot.

"Hello?" Ethan called out.

His voice was swallowed up in the night air.

They stepped closer. "Do you see anything?" Ethan whispered.

"No!"

Ethan's eyes were adjusting to the dark. He could see the outline of the Dumpster now. The top was open.

He put his hands on the rim. Tensing his muscles, he pulled himself slowly up.

*CLAAAANNNNNGGGG!*

Ethan fell to the blacktop. He scrambled to his feet and found himself shaking in Cecelia's arms.

A low voice resounded from within the Dumpster: *"Ha-ha-ha-HA-HA-HAAAAAAAA!"*

# 13

Ethan and Cecelia turned and ran.

"STOP RIGHT THERE...OR ELSE BEWARE!" the voice commanded.

Cecelia stopped short. "Wait a minute..." Hands on hips, she faced the Dumpster.

"Let's go!" Ethan urged.

"Come out!" Cecelia called to the Dumpster.

Ethan pulled her arm. "Look, I have a confession. I put the primordial soup into the spinach-garlic-garbanzo bean casserole, okay? And it made the stuff come to life, I know it. Even though it sounds stupid and Philomena thinks I'm crazy and it's scientifically impossible. *But I think the spinach has evolved into a monster!*"

Cecelia was ignoring him. "Hardy Fledermaus, is that you?"

"Awwwww, you spoiled it!" Hardy stepped from behind the Dumpster, cackling with laughter.

Ethan wanted to strangle him. "That was low, Hardy. Very low."

" 'The spinach has evolved into a monster!' I *love* it! Oh, that's great! Hoooooo-ha-ha-ha-ha!"

"Hardy, what are you doing here?" Cecelia demanded.

Hardy took a sheet of paper out of his back pocket. "I was bringing you a song I wrote. Imagine my surprise when I got to Roquefort Court! I couldn't believe who I saw. You and I are using the same muse!"

"Oh, Hardy, don't be a cerebrally underdeveloped miscreant," Cecelia said.

"That's 'dork,' in dumb-kid language," Hardy said to Ethan.

Ethan balled his fists. "I've had enough insults."

"Eeeek!" Hardy shrieked. "I'm sooooo scared."

He ran behind the Dumpster. It rolled forward a few inches.

"Hey, it's empty," Ethan said.

"Your brain?" Hardy said. "I could have told you that."

"The Dumpster," Ethan said, ignoring the comment. "It was full when we left school."

"Maybe the sanitation truck came," Cecelia suggested.

Ethan shook his head. "It always comes in the morning. I've seen it."

"So, it changed its schedule," Hardy said.

Ethan crouched down. The area around the Dumpster looked clean, except for a decaying banana peel to its left.

54

Beyond the banana peel was a used container of yogurt. And a bit farther, a pile of unidentifiable squashed food.

"Hungry?" Hardy asked. "You go ahead and eat here. Cecelia and I prefer the Double Helix."

"Cram it, Hardy," Cecelia and Ethan said together.

Ethan followed the food path into the ring of light. Now he could see it wasn't only bits of food. It was a slithery smear, leading from the Dumpster to the Ecobubble.

"What's this?" Cecelia asked.

"Gee, it sure is getting late," Hardy said. "Shouldn't we go?"

Ethan and Cecelia walked across the Astroturf path, following the slimy trail.

The Ecobubble door was shut. But the smear seemed to continue underneath it.

Ethan tried the knob, but it was locked tight.

"I wish we had a flashlight," Cecelia whispered.

Ethan pressed his face to the glass. "We may not need one."

Inside, the Ecobubble was glowing. But the light was not radiating down from a ceiling source. Instead, it seemed to be seeping upward from the floor.

"Wow," Cecelia gasped. "It's some sort of chemical fluorescence, perhaps caused by phosphor —"

"Shhhh," Ethan said. "Do you hear something?"

"N-n-no," Hardy replied. "But I feel it."

Ethan did, too. The Ecobubble walls were vibrating. The ground seemed to buzz beneath them.

"Uh, I sure could go for a Ballistic Banana Split," Hardy said.

"If only we could see . . ." Ethan said. Although the glow was intensifying, the glass walls were heavily misted.

"Ethan, this is spooky," Cecelia said. "Let's go."

"Okay, okay," Ethan replied. "But we have to tell Phil about this. She'll know what's going on."

They began walking away, at first slowly, then picking up speed.

The buzzing was louder now. The vibrating felt like a small earthquake.

"What's happening?" Cecelia asked.

*BOOOOOOOM!*

The blast knocked them all off their feet.

The Ecobubble burst outward in an explosion of glass and dirt.

Ethan squinted into the blinding light.

Something dark and green was hurtling toward them amidst the debris. Something the size of a tidal wave.

# 14

"**G**o!" Ethan pushed Cecelia to her feet.
*POP! POP!*

The glass was shattering behind them like gunshots.

Ethan and Cecelia scrambled toward the front of the school, right on Hardy's heels. They stopped by the front doors, shielded from the Ecobubble. Ethan was panting for breath.

"Are you all right?" he asked Cecelia.

"Barely," she replied.

"Now do you believe me?" Ethan asked.

"About what?" Cecelia replied.

"The green stuff! Shooting out of the Ecobubble! Didn't you see it?"

"What are you talking about?" Hardy asked.

"I didn't look back," Cecelia said. "It was probably plants."

"*It wasn't plants!*" Ethan insisted. "That's what I've been trying to tell you!"

"What else could it be?" Hardy asked.

"You're not still thinking about that spinach-garlic-garbanzo bean casserole?" Cecelia said.

"*Yes!*" Ethan began pacing. "It took over the Ecobubble. It must have fed on all the plants inside! And the soil! That must have been part of it. The stupid radioactive fast-grow soil! Oh, great, this is all we need!"

Hardy and Cecelia exchanged a look.

"I take back anything I ever said about you being normal," Hardy said.

Ethan was frantic. "We have to get out of here!"

Hardy grabbed his shoulders. "Krantz, please, chill in."

"Out."

"Whatever. Look, I always knew the Ecobubble was going to explode. All that methane and nitrogen inside — what a dumb idea. It was all Phil's fault. I tried to warn her."

"You did not," Cecelia said.

"Well, I was going to . . ." Hardy replied.

"Don't blame Phil for this!" Ethan snapped.

"Oops, sorry," Hardy said. "I didn't mean to insult your main cheese."

"Squeeze!" Ethan corrected him.

Hardy tightened his grip on Ethan's shoulders.

"Yeeow!" Ethan yelled. "Stop that!"

"You told me to squeeze."

*CRRRASSSHHHHH!*

The sound came from inside the school.

"How do you explain that, genius?" Ethan yelled.

Hardy shrugged. "Maybe Phil's in the john, breaking the time barrier. You know, like the sound barrier?"

"Hardy, you stuck-up geek —"

"Will you guys stop it!" Cecelia shouted. "We have to find a pay phone and call the police! I'll go south. Hardy, you go north. Ethan, head toward Main Street."

As Hardy and Cecelia tore off, Ethan spotted a small, yellow telephone cabinet attached to the wall of the school. Above it was the word EMERGENCY.

Ethan raced to the phone. It was old and rusted, made of thick metal. He yanked the handle hard, but the door wouldn't budge.

Planting his feet, Ethan grabbed the handle with both hands. He pulled again, with his whole body.

With a *snnnnap*, the handle came right off.

Ethan stumbled back. Now the phone's door had two jagged, rusted holes.

He stepped closer. The holes looked about finger width. He reached toward them.

*SSSHHHHHHUUURP!*

Two thick streams of green ooze gushed out, right toward Ethan's face!

# 15

"**Y**EEEEEEAGGHHH!"

Ethan was in mid-sprint when he ran into Hardy.

They both tumbled to the ground.

"Yeeow!" Hardy cried.

"*You don't believe me? Huh?*" Ethan was shrieking. He pointed back toward the emergency phone. "*Well, go take a look! Go ahead!*"

The yellow metal door was still closed. But the holes looked black and empty.

"Are you okay?" Cecelia was approaching them across the lawn now, looking concerned.

"Be careful!" Ethan warned, springing up. He walked slowly to the phone. "In there. Don't touch it!"

Hardy reached out. "It's just a phone!"

"*Stop!*" Ethan reached to grab Hardy's arm.

Too late.

Hardy inserted two fingers and pulled.

With a creak, the door opened.

"NOOOOOOO!" Ethan shouted.

"Will you calm down?" Cecelia said.

The phone inside was missing. In its place was a large hole, where it had once been hooked up to a cable.

"But — but I saw —" Ethan sputtered.

*Rrrrrrrrrr* . . . a distant siren sounded.

"I found a phone and called the police," Cecelia explained.

"You should have tried the mental hospital, too," Hardy said.

"But — but —" Ethan tried.

"You told us that already," Hardy remarked.

*I did see it,* Ethan thought. *I am not crazy.* "The Ecobubble! That will prove everything."

He stumbled to the side of the school to look.

*RRRRRRRRR* . . .

With lights flashing, a police car pulled up to the curb. Two officers jumped out: a bleary-eyed, dark-haired man and a tall, stocky blond woman.

"What's the problem?" said the policeman. "Someone been playing with the chemicals in the basement again?"

"It's not the basement," Hardy said. "It's the Ecobubble."

Ethan approached the corner of the school. He carefully looked around.

He went instantly numb with shock.

The Ecobubble was nothing more than a frame with empty panes. Inside, tables and flowerpot fragments lay all over the ground, surrounded by broken glass. A wisp of smoke curled upward and disappeared.

That was all. No slime. No giant green monster. Nothing.

The two police officers strolled up to Ethan. The woman let out a low whistle. "What were they *making* in there?"

Ethan ran toward the Ecobubble. "It was here . . . I saw it . . . it had to be . . ."

He didn't stop until he was in the midst of the debris. Not a trace of green was left. Not a leaf or stem. Beneath the strewn tables and equipment, the ground was bare.

He heard the jangling of key chains as the police officers ran toward him, followed by Hardy and Cecelia.

"It ate all the plants . . ." Ethan muttered to himself.

"What ate all the plants?" the policeman asked.

"The slime . . ." Ethan said.

"Uh, that's right, officers — *this lime*," Hardy blurted out. "You see, we used a large concentration of lime, which may have altered the acidity of the soil, thereby, uh . . ."

"Raising the autophagous capacity of the organic matter to dangerous levels," Cecelia improvised.

The two cops narrowed their eyes. "That doesn't make any sense," the woman said.

"What are your names again?" asked the man.

Ethan crouched low. He walked around the perimeter of the former Ecobubble, scanning the ground carefully.

Then he stopped. About fifteen feet from him, a wide, slimy trail led away from the edge of the barren ground.

Ethan's eyes followed it toward the school. The trail stopped at a basement window.

A window that had been smashed to pieces.

Ethan ran toward it.

"Hey, where do you think you're going?" the policewoman called out.

"It's in there . . ." Ethan cried.

The woman pointed Ethan toward the squad car. "And you're going in *there!* You kids have a lot of explaining to do at the station."

Ethan slumped across the lawn toward the police car. As he passed the ET indicator, he glanced at the gauge.

It was going wild.

# 16

"**H**rrrllllfcchh?"

"Phil? Wake up. It's me, Ethan."

"Ethan? What time is it?"

"Seven in the morning. Sorry, I had to call you."

"Don't tell me. Last night was a disaster."

"How did you know?"

"Just a guess. I'm sorry it turned out like that, Ethan. I tried to put in a good word for you."

"No! This isn't about Cecelia. This is a huge emergency! I spent an hour in the police station last night."

"Whaaaaat?"

"Listen, Phil. I hardly slept. I'm a total mess. You're the only person I can talk to about this. Just do me one favor — when I finish what I'm about to say, don't tell me I'm crazy."

"Okay."

"I saw something slither on the school floor yesterday. I tried to follow it, which was why I left you waiting. I figured it was a lizard. But just be-

64

fore you scared me, I spotted something green in the Dumpster. Anyway, last night, the Dumpster was empty. A trail of slime led to the Ecobubble, and everything inside it was glowing and rumbling. Then the whole thing exploded with spinach-garlic-garbanzo bean casserole — and everything inside had been eaten. By the time the police came, the casserole had oozed across the parking lot and into the school basement — and the ET indicator was going nuts."

"You're crazy."

"Phil, one of two things happened. One: The stuff I made *was* primordial soup. Something in the casserole brought it to life. When it went into the Ecobubble, it breathed the ancient atmosphere and got into the weird Eulenspiegel soil. It picked up whatever makes those plants grow so big and fierce. Now it's evolving and trying to take over the planet."

"And two?"

"I'm crazy."

"Who knows about this, Ethan?"

"No one. Hardy and Cecelia won't believe me. The cops thought I was making fun of them. They accused us of vandalizing the school. They said they'd call Sneed today."

"What about your parents? Do they know?"

"No."

"Weren't they suspicious when you came home late?"

65

"They didn't notice. They were still watching TV."

"Let's meet at the school, Ethan. I want to investigate this stuff myself."

"Sure."

"See you there."

" 'Bye."

# 17

The school's parking lot was almost empty. The only sound was the buzzing and crashing of a repair crew, working on the EMS basement windows.

Ethan looked at his watch. Seven thirty-two. Before long, the teachers would be arriving.

In the distance, he could see Philomena running across the parking lot. She was staring at the ruins of the Ecobubble.

"Oh, no . . ." she gasped.

"What did I tell you?" Ethan said.

He followed Phil into the dusty, debris-strewn area. She walked around slowly, gazing at the ground. Her face was sad and drawn. Kneeling down, she picked up a broken piece of pottery. "It's slimy."

"*Yesss!*" Ethan cried.

Phil sniffed it. "Definite traces of ammonia and spinach."

"Now do you believe me?"

67

"Yes and no." Phil began pacing. "We have to think about this . . ."

"What's to think? If this stuff takes over the town, we're dead meat! We have to get someone to believe us!"

"Maybe we can deal with it ourselves."

*"Phil, I don't believe you're saying this!"*

"Think of it, Ethan. Newspaper headlines: 'Primordial Soup Discovered by Brilliant Eulenspiegel Student and Her Friend —' "

Ethan raised an eyebrow. "Don't you mean '*His* Friend'?"

" 'Life Created in a Test Tube; Just Add Spinach and Garlic.' "

"Don't forget the garbanzo beans . . ."

"Ethan, we can become famous! The youngest winners of the Nobel Prize ever!"

"If we live long enough."

"You are so negative. Okay, say we have some form of primitive life. Some mutant giant amoeba or something. It can only do two things. Eat and grow. You see? We have nothing to be afraid of."

"Uh, Phil. I may not be a genius. But if something *grows* big enough, it can *eat* us. Am I right?"

"Ah, but we have one thing it doesn't — intelligence."

"Speak for yourself."

"Ethan, don't be so down on yourself. We're billions of years ahead of this thing. Come, let's conquer our enemy and save the school. It'll be good for your self-esteem."

As Phil ran toward the school, Ethan yelled, "Wait! What's our plan?"

"I'll think of something!"

Phil marched right up to the workers, who were clustered around a set of basement windows. "Step aside," she commanded. "I must enter the basement, in the service of science."

The workers turned. "Be my guest," said one of them.

Each basement window had thick metal bars across it.

"Scratch that idea," Ethan muttered.

"Follow me!" Phil took off like a shot.

Ethan followed her inside the school. The hallway had an early-morning musty, lemony smell. A few students and teachers were straggling in.

Ethan and Phil veered left past the auditorium. At the end of the hall, Mr. Schmutzkopf and two assistants were trying to open the door to the basement.

"What's going on?" Phil called out.

"It's stuck!" Mr. Schmutzkopf said.

"Use the elevator!" Ethan suggested.

"It's in the basement. Won't come up."

Ethan glanced at the elevator's digital readout. It was glowing "B."

*"There you are!"* a familiar voice boomed out.

Phil and Ethan whirled around. Mr. Sneed was huffing and puffing toward them, his face red.

"Uh-oh," Phil muttered.

*"Ethan Krantz, I want you in my office, pronto!"* Mr. Sneed roared.

"Mr. Sneed," Phil said, "I must inform you that a unique and potentially dangerous scientific opportunity lies directly below us, and —"

Mr. Sneed grabbed Ethan by the arm. "This does not involve you, Ms. Capstan. I'd advise that you stay away from this . . . this *vandal*. This juvenile delinquent! The police told me everything you said, Ethan — and I am shocked at you. Do you know how much that Ecobubble cost our school?"

"But I didn't touch it!" Ethan pleaded.

"Oh? I suppose some giant green blob did, right?"

"You saw it, too?"

*"That does it! March!"*

"Wait!" Phil called out. "Do you realize what you are doing to his feeling of self-worth?"

Mr. Sneed looked at her as if she'd lost her mind. "Philomena, can't you run along and . . . go have breakfast with Abraham Lincoln or something?"

"I will not be patronized," Phil said, holding her chin high. "If you take him, you take me, too!"

"Fine!" Mr. Sneed said.

He led them both to the administrative office.

Behind a long counter, school officials worked in tiny cubicles. In front of the counter, on the wall to the left, was a dark wooden door labeled PRINCI-PAL. Next to the door was a hard wooden bench.

"Stay here and don't move." Mr. Sneed stormed out into the hallway again, slamming the outer door behind him.

Phil and Ethan sat on the bench. "On any scientific matters, let me do the talking," Phil whispered.

"Thanks a lot," Ethan grunted.

A few moments later, Mr. Sneed returned with Hardy and Cecelia.

Hardy pointed to Ethan. "He did it!"

Ethan opened his mouth to answer back, but Phil put her hand over it. "My client refuses to speak on the grounds that it may incriminate him."

"I will find out the truth," Mr. Sneed said, with an evil glint in his eye. "I will see each of you in my office, one by one. Ethan first."

Mr. Sneed held open his door. Ethan slumped into the office.

"As his representative, I protest!" Phil said, jumping to her feet. "According to the bylaws of the Eulenspiegel Middle School, each student has the right to a fair hearing on matters of disciplinary action."

"What *bylaws*?" Hardy said.

"I'll show you," Phil said, reaching for a set of leather-bound books against a wall beside the counter.

Mr. Sneed let out a sigh of frustration. "I'll be right in," he said to Ethan. "Sit in the most uncomfortable chair."

He slammed the door. The arguing voices became muffled.

Ethan sank into an old metal-frame chair with a ripped cushion. Mr. Sneed's office was small and cramped. Behind him, enormous bowling trophies sat atop a small, dusty bookcase. Papers and folders were all over, piled on the desk, the file cabinets, and most other horizontal spaces. An overhead light in a waffle-pattern frame bathed the room in a harsh white light.

A steady stream of frigid air blew from the air-conditioning duct in the ceiling. Ethan slid the chair over to avoid the draft.

". . . And furthermore, young lady, this is not a court of law . . ." Mr. Sneed's voice carried in.

Ethan began pacing the room. *What can I possibly tell him?* he thought. The truth? Mr. Sneed would freak. He'd suspend Ethan for weeks. Maybe expel him.

Hmmmm. That didn't sound like a bad idea, actually.

But how would he explain that to his parents? And what other school would take him? One look at his permanent record and forget it.

Through the window, Ethan could see the shell of the Ecobubble. The workers were now cleaning up the mess, dumping it into huge buckets. They were smiling, joking around with each other. In the full light of day, everything looked so peaceful.

*Maybe it really was gas.*

The thought elbowed its way into Ethan's brain.

Since the cafeteria incident, no one else had seen the green stuff. No one but Ethan.

Maybe he hadn't been thinking straight. Sure, the explosion happened. Sure, the plants had vaporized and the basement windows had broken. But the blast could have caused all of that.

The slime? Lizards or squirrels, dragging garbage around. The stuck basement door and elevator? That kind of stuff happened all the time.

Pressure. That's what it was. The pressure of moving. Of being the stupidest kid in a school of geniuses. Couldn't people hallucinate under great stress?

This was all some kind of waking nightmare.

Had to be.

There was no slime. No monster.

He would tell the truth to Mr. Sneed. He had nothing to lose.

Ethan drew himself to his full height and faced the door.

He heard a dull clattering. At first he thought it was the doorknob.

But the noise was coming from above him.

73

From the air-conditioning duct.

He looked up. The metal vent was shaking. The stupid thing must have been turned up too high.

*Clinkety-clank-clank* . . .

The vent was rocking, bending. The screws were not going to hold it.

"Mr. Sneed?" Ethan called out.

*WHAM!* The vent crashed to the floor.

Out of the gaping hole, like a waterfall, poured a quivering mass of stringy green glop.

As soon as it hit the floor, it rose up. Billowing, oozing. Growing toward the ceiling like a great beast.

Ethan opened his mouth in a silent scream.

# 18

"**A**nd I'll have you know, in all my twenty-three years in Eulenspiegel, I've never seen such disrespect . . ." Mr. Sneed's voice rumbled on outside the door.

Ethan staggered backward.

The blob was bubbling. Soft brownish lumps popped to the surface, only to disappear into the boiling green mass.

It was fluid. Wet and slimy. And yet it seemed to be standing upright.

"Mi — Mis — M —" Ethan could not get the principal's name out of his dried-up throat.

Before Ethan's eyes, the blob began to change shape. It elongated. It narrowed at the top. Two extensions grew out of its sides.

Ethan groped behind him for the doorknob with his right hand.

The blob's right extension bent backward.

Ethan's hand smacked against the edge of a bookcase, and he pulled back in pain. "Ow!"

The blob's extension smacked against the trophy shelf. A huge bowling trophy smashed to the floor.

"L-l-look, I d-don't know what you are, b-b-but you have to leave me alone!" Ethan crouched low and stepped back toward the door. "See, I'm only twelve. I have my whole life ahead of me . . ."

The blob doubled over. Slowly it squirmed toward the opposite end of the room, making funny squeaking noises.

Ethan's eyes widened. "I don't believe this."

A small hole opened near the top of the blob. It began opening and closing. *"Raaa do-o-o-o reeeeeeer deeees . . ."*

"You're — you're imitating me!"

*"Yo — yo mimimimimi!"*

"NO-O-O-O-O-O!"

Ethan bolted out into the main room.

*WHAM!* He slammed the door behind him and kept going.

Mr. Sneed grabbed him by the arm. "Not so fast, Ethan."

"Let me go!" Ethan cried. "You don't understand. It's in there!"

"What's in there?" Mr. Sneed demanded.

*"The spinach casserole!"*

Mr. Sneed looked flabbergasted. "Funny, I ordered ham and eggs over easy, with a cup of warm Ovaltine. I don't know what has gotten into Mrs. Gastronome —"

*"It talks!"* Ethan pressed on.

"Young man," Mr. Sneed said, "you will not refer to Mrs. Gastronome as 'it'!"

Phil was on her feet. "I smell the casserole."

"I do, too," said Cecelia.

"Could be the boys' room across the hall," Hardy commented.

*"We have to get out of here!"* Ethan shouted. *"It's in the air-conditioning!"*

"Of all the impudent tricks!" Mr. Sneed thundered. "How on earth did you get spinach-garlic-garbanzo bean casserole in the cooling system?"

*"I* didn't!" Ethan said.

"I suppose it got there by itself?" Mr. Sneed yanked Ethan toward the door.

Ethan dug his heels in. "Please don't do this, Mr. Sneed!"

"I'll bring you up on charges, Mr. Sneed!" Phil shouted, pulling Ethan's other arm. "This is unlawful physical contact, as defined by the State of New Mexico civil code —"

Mr. Sneed grabbed the doorknob.

Hardy and Cecelia scrambled to their feet to get a better look.

"DO-O-O-ON'T!" Ethan shrieked.

Behind him, the hallway door flew open. "Mr. Sneed!" called Mr. Schmutzkopf. "Something smells pretty bad out here."

Mr. Sneed looked over his shoulder. "I have the problem under control."

"No, you don't," Mr. Schmutzkopf replied. "The kids and teachers can't stand it. They're leaving."

He flung the hallway door open. In rushed the sounds of loud shouting and scuffling feet.

"What the — ?" Mr. Sneed let go of Ethan. He and Phil both tumbled to the floor.

Mr. Sneed went to the hallway door and gazed out. Kids were dashing right and left, grabbing stuff from their lockers.

Through the outer office windows, Ethan could see students and teachers running across the school lawn.

"How much casserole did you put in there?" Mr. Sneed asked.

"Play along," Phil whispered.

"Uh — a lot!" Ethan improvised. "A whole garbage barrel full. Oh, wow, do I feel guilty!"

"Guess you'll officially have to evacuate the school!" Phil said.

Mr. Sneed sighed. "I suppose, but I can't do that without consulting the superintendent."

He headed back to his inner office.

Ethan flung himself against the door, arms wide.

"Allow me!" Phil said. She jumped over the counter and grabbed the P.A. mike off a nearby table. *"Attention all Eulenspiegel students. School is officially over for the day! Go home! Better yet, leave town!"*

"Good-bye!" the secretaries all sang out, scurrying away.

"GIVE ME THAT!" Mr. Sneed roared, his face pinched with anger.

He tried to leap over the counter, but his belly jammed against the edge. He rolled to the other side, thumping onto the floor.

"Crazy," Hardy said, shaking his head. "The whole school is certifiably nutzoid."

Now the smell was overpowering. Ethan's eyes began to tear from the stench. He ran to the hallway door. "Come on!"

"Just a minute," Cecelia said. "I want to see what's in here."

Before Ethan could protest, Cecelia reached for Mr. Sneed's office door.

With a firm tug, she pulled it open.

Ethan could feel the blood draining from his face.

Mr. Sneed peered over the counter and into his office. He went chalk white.

"No," he murmured. "NO!"

# 19

"*My trophy!*" Mr. Sneed wailed. On the verge of tears, he ran into the office and knelt by the broken pieces of his bowling trophy. "You don't know how much work went into this!"

Ethan crept closer. Hardy, Cecelia, and Phil were right behind him.

The air-conditioning vent was on the floor, bent.

Ethan frantically scanned the room, looking behind every desk and cabinet, every pile of paper.

But the blob was gone.

"That championship night was pure magic," Mr. Sneed was sobbing.

"Man, does it stink," Hardy said. He went to the windows and pulled one open.

"Where did it go?" Phil asked.

Ethan caught a warm drip on his forehead. He gasped and jumped back.

Looking up, he saw the gaping square of the ceiling duct. "Back up through there?"

Phil dragged a chair under the duct and climbed up.

"Four strikes in a row..." Mr. Sneed murmured, "followed by a spare. The crowd went wild..."

"Eeeew!" Cecelia cried. She lifted her sneaker from the carpet, and a gob of green slime came with it.

"Who-o-oa," Hardy said. "It *is* the casserole!"

Ethan threw his arms in the air. "Hallelujah!"

"I don't know why you're so happy," Cecelia shot back. "Do you know how much these shoes cost?"

"I mean, hallelujah, you believe me!" Ethan said. "Hallelujah, I'm not crazy!"

Phil was now on tiptoes on the chair, her head in the ceiling vent. "Hey!" she called out. "It's glowigg id here."

"Glowigg?" Hardy repeated.

Phil looked down. She was pinching her nose. "You'd soud like this, too, Flederbaus, if your doze was id this stedch."

"Mr. Sneed," Ethan said, "where do the air-conditioning ducts lead?"

"The basement," Mr. Sneed replied absently, still hunched over his trophy. "That's where we were, the basement... no one predicted we'd out-bowl the West Gallup Guttersnipes and rise to first place..."

"We have to get down there," Phil said.

"How?" Hardy said. "Dynamite through the locked door? Go fishing for the elevator?"

"Even if we do," Cecelia said. "Then what?"

"We're gobbled up for lunch, that's what," Ethan said. "Either that or we're used as guinea pigs. That . . . that *thing* tried to copy everything I was doing!"

"You must have been flattered," Hardy remarked.

"I say we go home, pack up, and move to someplace far away and safer," Ethan said. "Like New York City."

Phil was pacing the floor. "What if this . . . *organism* has been genetically programmed to accelerate its evolution?" she said. "What if it leaps a billion years in a single bound? What if it develops superior intelligence?"

"Don't worry," Hardy said. "It was imitating Ethan."

"Hardy, can't you take anything seriously?" Cecelia snapped.

"I say we try to defeat it," Phil said. "Defeat it before its power is unleashed on the world!"

"Yeah? How?" Hardy asked.

"I'm not sure," Phil replied. "But we're scientists. First we observe, then we get to work. We need a sample of this stuff. Something we can analyze in a lab. The only way we can defeat this is to understand it."

Phil gave Ethan a level stare.

Hardy and Cecelia both looked confused and scared. But no one in the room besides Ethan had actually seen the creature. No one but Ethan had smelled it up close, seen its attempts at human behavior.

How long would it be before someone else did see it? How big would it grow? When would it be ready to emerge from the basement? To show itself to the world?

Ethan nodded. "I'm with you, Phil."

"Me, too," Cecelia said.

"I guess you can count me in, too," Hardy agreed.

"Counted out, that's what we were," Mr. Sneed was muttering. "Until the final frame, when Elmer Sneed toed the line, eyeing the pins . . ."

Ethan, Phil, Hardy, and Cecelia ran out together. Their footsteps clattered down the hallway, which was now empty.

They stopped at the basement door.

Hammers, torches, screwdrivers, and a few other tools had been abandoned on the floor. The metal door was badly dented around the edges.

Ethan tried to turn the knob. "It won't budge."

"Duh," Hardy said.

"Now what?" Cecelia asked.

"Knock," Phil replied.

Hardy burst out laughing. "I like that. That's funny."

Phil lifted her right hand and rapped sharply on the door.

*PONG! PONG! PONG!*

The sounds echoed dully, then faded.

"Gee, that was a great idea," Hardy remarked.

Ethan picked up a crowbar. But just as he reached for the door, a noise stopped him.

A high-pitched, squeaky voice.

*"COMINNNNNNG!"*

Slowly the doorknob began to turn.

# 20

Ethan's body was shaking. He unlocked his knees and backed away.

Phil reached down and picked up a hammer. Ethan gripped his crowbar tightly and handed Hardy a propane torch. Cecelia took a screwdriver.

"Uh, got to go!" Hardy said. "See, my dad and mom are preparing a big dinner. You're all invited..."

*Eeeeeee...*

The door inched open.

Hardy's teeth were chattering.

Ethan braced himself.

A dim greenish glow shone from below. It barely lit up the stairwell.

The empty stairwell.

"How does it do that?" Ethan said under his breath.

*"Co-o-o-ome i-i-i-innn..."* the voice squeaked.

"Uh, th-thanks for the i-i-invita-ta-tion," Hardy stammered. "B-b-but — "

"*Y-o-o-o we-e-ellcome . . .*"

Phil took a step forward.

"Don't go near it!" Ethan exclaimed.

"Why?" Phil said. "It didn't do anything to you."

"Phil . . . I don't know about this . . ." Cecelia said.

"I do!" Hardy said. "I'm out of here!"

"*No-o-o,*" the voice continued. "*Sta-a-ay . . .*"

Hardy froze.

"How did it learn so many words?" Ethan murmured.

"*Beeeeen li-i-i-issstening . . .*" the voice replied.

"Come on, guys," Phil said, stepping to the top of the stairs.

Ethan swallowed deeply. He couldn't let her do this alone.

He walked up beside her and looked down. A trail of spinach-y guck dribbled down the wooden steps into a swirling, grayish-green mist.

Ethan narrowed his eyes. "Where are you?" he called.

"*Co-o-o-ome do-o-own . . .*"

Hardy laughed. "Yeah, right. Like we're really going to just walk down there."

"Show us yourself!" Ethan demanded.

"*Tooooo sca-a-ared!*"

"Aha!" Phil said. "It's more frightened than we are!"

"Don't forget," Cecelia said, "we burned seven barrels of it."

"Should have been eight," Hardy muttered.

"We won't hurt you!" Ethan called out. "We just want to understand what you are!"

"*U-u-us tooo . . .*" the voice answered.

"Good, Ethan," Cecelia whispered.

"This is a piece of cake," Ethan replied with a smile. Then he shouted: "Okay, listen. Just curious, but could you spare a small piece of yourself?"

"*Whyyyy?*"

"Well, you see, you're such a fantastic and unusual life-form to us," Ethan explained, "we'd just love to find out exactly what you're made of."

"On behalf of all the students in Eulenspiegel," Phil murmured under her breath. "I proudly accept this Nobel Prize . . ."

"*Heeere weee co-o-o-ome . . .*"

Ethan let his crowbar fall to the floor. "Come on, guys, no tools. Let's show it how friendly we are."

Hardy's knees were shaking. "Are you sure this is the right thing to do?"

"Hardy Fledermaus, are you chicken?" Cecelia asked.

"Me?" Hardy snorted. "Chicken?"

From below, a rumbling began.

Hardy dropped his torch. "Buck-buck-buck-buck . . ."

Ethan, Cecelia, and Phil all stood at the top of

the stairs, holding hands. "It told us it would cooperate," Phil said. "So we have nothing to fear."

"Fear is my middle name," Hardy said.

"Go home, Hardy, if you're such a baby," Cecelia said.

With a big sigh, Hardy shuffled next to Cecelia and clutched her hand.

The basement's green glow began to dim. A black shadow came slowly into view. Ethan felt Cecelia's hand tense up. "Steady," he said.

Ethan could see the glob now, pushing out of the shadow.

Intense waves of spinach, garlic, and garbanzo bean stink invaded the air, mixed with ammonia, dirt, and peculiar chemicals.

The blob began rolling up the stairs toward them.

It was enormous, completely blacking out the green glow. The stairwell sagged under the weight. Flecks of green moisture flung upward toward Ethan and his friends.

"Gross," Cecelia muttered.

"Okay, you can stop now," Ethan said, covering his face.

"It's not listening," Phil said.

"Oh my lord . . ." Cecelia whispered. "It's coming for us!"

"Mommyyyyy!" Hardy whimpered.

"That's enough!" Ethan shouted. "You can . . . *STO-O-O-OP!*"

# 21

"*H*ELLLLLP!*"

Hardy ran down the hall.

Ethan started after him. "Come on!"

But Phil was rigid. "The-square-of-the-hypotenuse-of-a-right-triangle-is-equal-to-the-sum-of-the-squares-of-its-sides . . ." she mumbled.

"This is no time for algebra!" Ethan yelled.

"Geometry!" Phil replied. "It's — it's robbing our brains! I can feel it. It's trying to find out everything — the-biochemical-conversion-of-matter-to-energy-in-the-form-of-adenosine-triphosphate-is-accomplished-in-the-Krebs-Cycle-by-the-breakdown-of-carbohydrates — *I can't stop!*"

"Momentum-is-the-product-of-velocity-and-matter . . ." Cecelia was saying. "*Help!*"

Phil gritted her teeth. "*Try not to give in, Ethan!*"

Ethan could feel a funny buzzing in his head, but that was it. "I don't need to!" he cried. "There's not enough inside my brain to take! Let's go!"

Gripping Cecelia's and Phil's hands, he ran.

They stumbled along beside him, spouting science gibberish.

Ethan looked over his shoulder. The blob rumbled to the top of the stairs and came rolling after them.

He picked up speed, darting around the nearest corner.

*"Freeze!"*

Hardy was standing in the middle of the hallway with a fire extinguisher.

*FIIIIIIIISHHHHHH!*

White foam gushed out, coating the walls and floor.

"Sorry! I thought you were the blob!" Hardy said. "How do you stop this thing?"

"Who-o-oa!" Ethan slid on the foam. He let go of Phil and Cecelia.

Flailing their arms and legs, all three of them fell to the floor.

Hardy flung the extinguisher away. He reached down and pulled Cecelia to her feet. "Let's go!"

"Not without Ethan and Phil!" she screamed.

*SHHHKKLLUUUUURRRP!*

The blob oozed around the corner, sliming the walls and ceiling. *"Mo-o-o-o-ore!"* came its squeaky cry.

"Come on!" Hardy cried, pulling Cecelia away.

Ethan could feel the sticky warmth of the blob

as it approached. Quickly he glanced the other way, to the edge of the foam patch. Only about five feet away.

He scrambled to his feet but slipped again.

"Gravitational-acceleration-is-a-constant-which-is-expressed-as —" Phil droned. *"No! Leave me alone!"*

The blob descended upon Phil, dripping and hissing.

Ethan dropped to his side. He rolled.

At the edge of the foam, he stood up. *"Take my hand!"* he commanded.

Phil lunged toward him. Ethan grabbed her hand and pulled her — just as the blob settled over the foam.

*"MO-O-O-RE!"* The blob sounded like a greedy baby now.

Ethan looked up the hall. Hardy and Cecelia were booking. Almost to the cafeteria door. A few more yards, and they'd reach the side exit.

Ethan and Phil closed ground fast. They were almost to the boys' room now . . .

*Shhhhhhpannnnng!*

A section of the blob shot ahead. It curved around Hardy and Cecelia like a slimy fist.

"YEEEAAAAAGH!" They leaped away into the cafeteria, screaming.

"CECELIA!" Ethan shouted.

"EEEEEETHAAAAN!" she shrieked back.

He tried to run after her. But he couldn't.

His way was blocked by the blob. It was whipping around, trying to trap him and Phil.

"This way!" Phil urged.

Ethan felt himself being pulled by the hand. He stumbled through the boys' bathroom doorway.

Phil slammed the door shut.

"We're safe!" she exclaimed, panting for breath.

*SMMMMMMACK!* The door flew off its hinges and hit the tile floor.

Ethan raced to the windows and yanked one open. It only yielded about five inches.

"Any-two-objects-will-exhibit-an-equal-and-opposite-force-on-one-another — *HELP!*" Phil pleaded.

Ethan took her arm.

The blob advanced. Its fumes invaded Ethan's nostrils. He backed away, looking around frantically for escape.

The ceiling vent. Too high.

The upper windows. Barred and locked.

Nothing. No way out.

Now the blob was expanding, approaching from all sides, cornering them . . .

"*Mo-o-o-ore!*" it creaked.

". . . wave-particle-duality . . ." Phil was mumbling.

Ethan backed away, past the sinks . . .

His foot banged against the metal frame of a

stall door. He moved slightly to the left and backed in, clutching onto Phil.

The blob pressed against the open stall doorway, blocking Ethan and Phil. Permanently.

"No!" shouted Ethan.

"... inertial-frames ..." Phil droned.

*"MO-O-O-O-O-ORE!"*

Ethan was trapped. His back was to the wall. The slimy blob was bubbling over the stall walls, lowering onto them, cutting off all light. He crouched down. His elbow made contact with something cold and metallic.

*"NO-O-O-O-O-O!"*

The scream ripped up through his body.

The last sound Ethan heard was a swirling rush of liquid, as the blob closed darkly around him.

# 22

*QUOOOOOOOOOOOOOOSH!*

The sound was deafening. Ethan closed his eyes and gritted his teeth. His life ran through his brain like a home video: Frodo's birth . . . sixth-grade graduation . . . the move to Eulenspiegel . . . seeing Cecelia for the first time . . . the blob . . .

The blob.

It wasn't pressing against him.

It also didn't smell as bad.

Ethan's eyes flickered open.

He was in the boys' bathroom, all right. But outside the stall. Against the opposite wall.

He gazed around. The walls and floor were sparkling clean. He went to the bathroom door, opened it, and looked out.

A slight buzzing echoed distantly.

Voices. Human voices. The kind you heard in the middle of the school day.

And still no blob.

Ethan staggered back into the bathroom.

*QUOOOOOOOOOOOOOOSH!*

The horrible swirling sound suddenly stopped. Ethan realized what it was.

A flushing toilet. Behind a closed stall door.

With a loud *whack*, the door crashed open.

Out stepped Philomena, wearing a hat and beard.

"Ethan?" she said.

"Phil?"

Grinning wide, Phil unhooked her beard and threw off her hat. "You did it!"

"Did what — how —?" Ethan spluttered. "Where's the blob?"

"What's today's date, Ethan?"

"September seventh, of course, but —"

"Are you sure?"

Ethan glanced at his watch. He pressed the toggle button until it showed the date.

It read SEP 6.

"It's . . . yesterday," Ethan said.

"At the exact moment we met here." Phil jumped into the air. "Ya-hoooo! Ethan, I'm proud of you. How did you know the exact flush-lever pressure? Not to mention the precise duration equivalent of twenty-four hours?"

"You mean . . ." Ethan pointed to the toilet. "That's real?"

Phil nodded. "Naturally."

"I — I flushed, and we traveled backward in —?"

"Ethan, quick, where's that primordial soup?"

95

Ethan reached into his rear pocket. The test tube was there. Still stoppered. "I don't believe this . . ."

Phil looked to the door. "If I remember correctly, we should be receiving a visitor right about now."

Slowly the door swung open. Hardy peeked in. His face was drained of color. "Hi, guys. Are you . . . okay?"

"Peachy," Ethan replied.

"What happened?" Hardy pressed on. "The blob was here. And we were there. And now I'm here. And —"

*RRRRRING!*

The end-of-the-period bell rang.

"We'll explain later," Phil said. "First we need to find Cecelia."

They raced out of the bathroom. Ethan held onto the test tube tightly.

Just inside the cafeteria door, Cecelia was leaning against the wall. She was gazing into the room, stunned.

"Cecelia!" Ethan called out.

*"Ethan!"* She threw her arms around him.

Out of the corner of his eye, he spotted Hardy's glowering face.

It didn't bother Ethan a bit.

"Where's the blob?" Cecelia asked.

"It doesn't exist yet," Phil replied.

Ethan held up his test tube. "And it never will."

"How — ?" Cecelia began.

"Come," Ethan said, taking her hand. "We need to get rid of this stuff for good."

As Ethan led them all back to the bio lab, he carefully explained everything to Cecelia and Hardy.

As they approached the lab, Mr. Mosswort was briskly walking away. They hid around a corner until he was gone, then ran inside.

The lab was empty. Ethan raced to the fume hood. Under it was a Bunsen burner.

He lit the burner and turned on the hood to maximum. The internal fan began to whoosh, drawing the flame higher into the duct.

"Hold your noses," Ethan said.

He unstoppered the test tube, then held it over the flame.

Slowly the grotesque mixture began to bubble. Greenish smoke twined upward. As it left the lip of the tube, it carried swiftly into the updraft.

Hardy ran to an open window and put his head out. "I can see it!" he cried.

Phil and Cecelia joined him.

Ethan held the tube steadily until the entire mixture had disappeared into the dark fume hood, leaving only a small, burned residue. Then he raced to Cecelia's side and looked out.

The last traces of dark-green smoke billowed out of a wall vent. They lifted lazily upward into the cloudy sky.

"It's gone," he said under his breath. "We killed it before it could multiply."

When he looked back down, Cecelia was beaming at him. "Thanks, Ethan."

"It was nothing," Ethan said.

"Cut the mush," Hardy grumbled. "Come on, let's eat. I'm starving."

Phil put an arm around his shoulder. "I hear the main choice today is really great. Spinach something. Your dad makes it."

Hardy went pale. He sat down on a lab stool. "On second thought, I think I'll sit this one out."

# Epilogue

A date.

Ethan couldn't believe Cecelia had asked him. Right there in the cafeteria, during lunch.

Well, okay, a double date. Hardy and Phil were coming, too. But that was cool.

Ethan paced in front of the school. The day was over. Nothing unusual had happened. Lunch period had ended quietly, and no one had touched the spinach-garlic-garbanzo bean casserole. After lunch, Ethan had checked. The stuff was sitting harmlessly in its steam-table tray.

"We'll probably give it to Mr. Schmutzkopf," Mrs. Gastronome had said. "He needs mortar for a brick job."

"Hi!"

Ethan spun around at the sound of Cecelia's voice. Behind her were Hardy and Phil.

"Yo . . . we are party mammals!" Hardy bellowed.

"Animals," Ethan corrected him.

A crack of thunder sounded in the distance.

"Weird," Phil said. "It never rains in Eulenspiegel."

"We'd better hurry," Ethan said. "How do you want to celebrate?"

"*Return of the Blob Four* is playing at the cineplex," Hardy suggested.

"Nahhh," Phil said. "I like make-believe better."

Ethan and his friends jogged in the direction of the mall, talking and laughing.

Soon rain began falling from the dark clouds. Out of the corner of his eye, Ethan watched it seep slowly into the dry Eulenspiegel soil.

It took him a while to notice its color.

Green.

Dark green.

# About the Author

Peter Lerangis attended John W. Dodd Junior High School in Freeport, New York, where most of the time he ate bag lunches. He survived and eventually earned a degree in biochemistry at Harvard College, where one morning his cafeteria actually served bananas wrapped in ham with cheese sauce.

As a singer, Peter was personally removed by Seiji Ozawa from performing a solo with the Boston Symphony. As an actor, he spent a week in a Broadway show as an understudy for an understudy. These were two reasons he became a writer.

Peter has also written the strange *Spring Fever* and its equally strange sequel, *Spring Break*.

At the moment he is hard at work on his next book, *The Attack of the Killer Potatoes*.

# GET
# Goosebumps®
## by R.L. Stine

| | | | |
|---|---|---|---|
| ❏ BAB45365-3 | #1 | Welcome to Dead House | $3.99 |
| ❏ BAB45366-1 | #2 | Stay Out of the Basement | $3.99 |
| ❏ BAB45367-X | #3 | Monster Blood | $3.99 |
| ❏ BAB45368-8 | #4 | Say Cheese and Die! | $3.99 |
| ❏ BAB45369-6 | #5 | The Curse of the Mummy's Tomb | $3.99 |
| ❏ BAB49445-7 | #10 | The Ghost Next Door | $3.99 |
| ❏ BAB49450-3 | #15 | You Can't Scare Me! | $3.99 |
| ❏ BAB47742-0 | #20 | The Scarecrow Walks at Midnight | $3.99 |
| ❏ BAB47743-9 | #21 | Go Eat Worms! | $3.99 |
| ❏ BAB47744-7 | #22 | Ghost Beach | $3.99 |
| ❏ BAB47745-5 | #23 | Return of the Mummy | $3.99 |
| ❏ BAB48354-4 | #24 | Phantom of the Auditorium | $3.99 |
| ❏ BAB48355-2 | #25 | Attack of the Mutant | $3.99 |
| ❏ BAB48350-1 | #26 | My Hairiest Adventure | $3.99 |
| ❏ BAB48351-X | #27 | A Night in Terror Tower | $3.99 |
| ❏ BAB48352-8 | #28 | The Cuckoo Clock of Doom | $3.99 |
| ❏ BAB48347-1 | #29 | Monster Blood III | $3.99 |
| ❏ BAB48348-X | #30 | It Came from Beneath the Sink | $3.99 |
| ❏ BAB48349-8 | #31 | The Night of the Living Dummy II | $3.99 |
| ❏ BAB48344-7 | #32 | The Barking Ghost | $3.99 |
| ❏ BAB48345-5 | #33 | The Horror at Camp Jellyjam | $3.99 |
| ❏ BAB48346-3 | #34 | Revenge of the Lawn Gnomes | $3.99 |
| ❏ BAB48340-4 | #35 | A Shocker on Shock Street | $3.99 |
| ❏ BAB56873-6 | #36 | The Haunted Mask II | $3.99 |
| ❏ BAB56874-4 | #37 | The Headless Ghost | $3.99 |
| ❏ BAB56875-2 | #38 | The Abominable Snowman of Pasadena | $3.99 |
| ❏ BAB56876-0 | #39 | How I Got My Shrunken Head | $3.99 |
| ❏ BAB56877-9 | #40 | Night of the Living Dummy III | $3.99 |
| ❏ BAB56878-7 | #41 | Bad Hare Day | $3.99 |
| ❏ BAB56879-5 | #42 | Egg Monsters from Mars | $3.99 |
| ❏ BAB56880-9 | #43 | The Beast from the East | $3.99 |
| ❏ BAB56881-7 | #44 | Say Cheese and Die--Again! | $3.99 |
| ❏ BAB56882-5 | #45 | Ghost Camp | $3.99 |
| ❏ BAB56883-3 | #46 | How to Kill a Monster | $3.99 |
| ❏ BAB56884-1 | #47 | Legend of the Lost Legend | $3.99 |

---

### GOOSEBUMPS PRESENTS

| | | |
|---|---|---|
| ❏ BAB74586-7 | Goosebumps Presents TV Episode #1<br>The Girl Who Cried Monster | $3.99 |
| ❏ BAB74587-5 | Goosebumps Presents TV Episode #2<br>The Cuckoo Clock of Doom | $3.99 |
| ❏ BAB74588-3 | Goosebumps Presents TV Episode #3<br>Welcome to Camp Nightmare | $3.99 |
| ❏ BAB74589-1 | Goosebumps Presents TV Episode #4<br>Return of the Mummy | $3.99 |

| | | |
|---|---|---|
| ☐ BAB62836-4 | Tales to Give You Goosebumps<br>Book & Light Set Special Edition #1 | $11.95 |
| ☐ BAB26603-9 | More Tales to Give You Goosebumps<br>Book & Light Set Special Edition #2 | $11.95 |
| ☐ BAB74150-4 | Even More Tales to Give You Goosebumps<br>Book and Boxer Shorts Pack Special Edition #3 | $14.99 |

────────── GIVE YOURSELF GOOSEBUMPS ──────────

| | | |
|---|---|---|
| ☐ BAB55323-2 | Give Yourself Goosebumps #1:<br>Escape from the Carnival of Horrors | $3.99 |
| ☐ BAB56645-8 | Give Yourself Goosebumps #2:<br>Tick Tock, You're Dead | $3.99 |
| ☐ BAB56646-6 | Give Yourself Goosebumps #3:<br>Trapped in Bat Wing Hall | $3.99 |
| ☐ BAB67318-1 | Give Yourself Goosebumps #4:<br>The Deadly Experiments of Dr. Eeek | $3.99 |
| ☐ BAB67319-X | Give Yourself Goosebumps #5:<br>Night in Werewolf Woods | $3.99 |
| ☐ BAB67320-3 | Give Yourself Goosebumps #6:<br>Beware of the Purple Peanut Butter | $3.99 |
| ☐ BAB67321-1 | Give Yourself Goosebumps #7:<br>Under the Magician's Spell | $3.99 |
| ☐ BAB84765-1 | Give Yourself Goosebumps #8:<br>The Curse of the Creeping Coffin | $3.99 |
| ☐ BAB84766-X | Give Yourself Goosebumps #9:<br>The Knight in Screaming Armor | $3.99 |
| ☐ BAB53770-9 | The Goosebumps Monster Blood Pack | $11.95 |
| ☐ BAB50995-0 | The Goosebumps Monster Edition #1 | $12.95 |
| ☐ BAB60265-9 | Goosebumps Official Collector's Caps<br>Collecting Kit | $5.99 |
| ☐ BAB73906-9 | Goosebumps Postcard Book | $7.95 |
| ☐ BAB73902-6 | The 1997 Goosebumps 365 Scare-a-Day Calendar | $8.95 |
| ☐ BAB73907-7 | The Goosebumps 1997 Wall Calendar | $10.99 |

- - - - - - - - - - - - - - - - - - - - - - - - - - - - - - - - - - - - - - - - -

### Scare me, thrill me, mail me GOOSEBUMPS now!

Available wherever you buy books, or use this order form. Scholastic Inc., P.O. Box 7502,
2931 East McCarty Street, Jefferson City, MO 65102

Please send me the books I have checked above. I am enclosing $_____ (please add
$2.00 to cover shipping and handling). Send check or money order—no cash or C.O.D.s please.

Name _____Age _____

Address _____

City_____State/Zip _____

Please allow four to six weeks for delivery. Offer good in the U.S. only. Sorry, mail orders are not available to residents of Canada. Prices subject to change.